Once, long ago, by the shore of a large lake, there lived an old man and his three daughters.

The oldest was mean and cruel. The next was nasty and proud.

But the youngest was gentle and kind and very beautiful.

When the father was hunting in the forest, the older two would beat their younger sister and tear her clothes and push her in the mud so she was always dirty.

And that was why everyone called her "Little Dirty Face."

When the father came home from hunting, he would ask her why she was so dirty.

Her sisters would say she wouldn't listen to them and would rather play in the mud than do her chores. And the father would punish Little Dirty Face and send her to bed crying.

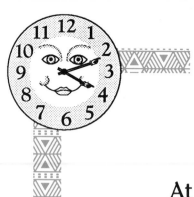

At the far end of the lake there was a beautiful wigwam, where there lived the Great Chief and his sister.

Although people could talk to the Great Chief, no one knew what he looked like. He was invisible.

No one could see him except his sister.
Things stayed that way for many years.
Then, one spring, his sister announced
that the Great Chief had decided to
marry.

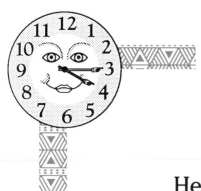

He didn't care whom he married. He would marry any girl in the tribe as long as she could do one thing — see him!

Every girl in the tribe was sure that she would be the one to see him.

Especially Little Dirty Face's two sisters. They dressed up in their best buckskin dresses and put on their shiniest beads and their most beautifully embroidered moccasins, ready to see the Great Chief.

But first they spoke to Little Dirty Face: "You stay here. You're too dirty to see the Chief."

Like the other village
maidens, the two mean
sisters went to the
Great Chief's wigwam.
And when the Chief's
sister asked them if
they could see the
Great Chief, the
oldest cried she
could see him:
"He wears a
white eagle
feather. He pulls
a sled with a
green strap."

The second sister shouted that she could see him too: "He wears a brown owl feather. He pulls a sled with a red strap."

Unknown to her sisters, poor Little Dirty Face put on her best clothes and borrowed her father's moccasins.

She was still ragged and dirty, because she had no soap to wash herself, but she went to the Chief's wigwam anyway. And when the Chief's sister asked her what she saw, she replied with shining eyes that she could see the Chief.

"He isn't wearing feathers."

Then the Chief's sister asked her, "What about the sled strap?" and she replied, "It's a beautiful rainbow."

The Chief's sister led Little Dirty Face
to the wigwam and bathed her with
dew until the dirt and scratches had all
disappeared from her face. Her skin
became soft and lovely. Her hair grew
long and shiny.

And when the Great Chief, no longer
invisible, saw Little Dirty Face, he
smiled and said gently,
"So we have found each other."
And she answered, "Yes."